Tony's Trip and the Letter T

Alphabet Friends

by Cynthia Klingel and Robert B. Noyed

The
Child's
World®

The Child's World®

Published in the United States of America
by The Child's World®
P.O. Box 326
Chanhassen, MN 55317-0326
800-599-READ
www.childsworld.com

The Child's World®: Mary Berendes, Publishing Director

Editorial Directions, Inc.: E. Russell Primm, Editorial
Director; Emily Dolbear, Line Editor; Ruth Martin,
Editorial Assistant; Linda S. Koutris, Photo Researcher
and Selector

Photographs ©: Corbis: Cover & 9; Jeff Tautrim/Brand X
Pictures/Picture Quest; Tim Hall/Photodisc/Picture Quest:
13; Andrew Bret Wallis/Photodisc/Getty Images: 14;
Photodisc/Getty Images: 17; Mark Cooper/Corbis: 18;
Stefanie Hafner/Photodisc/Getty Images: 21.

Library of Congress Cataloging-in-Publication Data
Klingel, Cynthia Fitterer.
  Tony's trip and the letter T / by Cynthia Klingel and
Robert B. Noyed.
    p. cm. — (Alphabet readers)
Summary: A simple story about a boy named Tony and
his visit to a toy store introduce the letter "t".
  ISBN 1-59296-110-X (Library Bound : alk. paper)
  [1. Toy stores—Fiction. 2. Alphabet.] I. Noyed, Robert
B., ill. II. Title. III. Series.
  PZ7.K6798To 2003
  [E]—dc21   2003006610

Note to parents and educators:
The first skill children acquire before becoming successful readers is individual letter recognition. The Alphabet Friends series has been created with the needs of young learners in mind. Each engaging book begins by showing the difference between the capital letter and the lowercase letter. In each of the books on the vowels and the consonants c and g, children are introduced to the different sounds that the letter can make. Finally, children see that the letters can be found at the beginning of a word, in the middle of a word, and in most cases, at the end of a word.

Following the introduction, children meet their Alphabet Friends. The friend in each story encounters many words that include the featured letter of that book. Each noun that begins with the title letter is highlighted in red with the initial letter of the word in bold. Above the word is a rebus drawing that establishes a strong picture cue.

At the end of each book, we have included three words lists. Can your young learners find all the words in each book with the title letter in them?

Let's learn about the letter **T.**

The letter **T** can look like this: **T.**

The letter **T** can also look like this: **t.**

The letter t can be at the beginning of a word, like toy.

toy

The letter t can be in the middle of a word, like postcard.

postcard

The letter **t** can be at the

end of a word, like quilt.

quil**t**

Tony is taking a trip to visit Aunt Tess in

the city. She is taking Tony to the toy store.

They will have a terrific time!

Aunt Tess is thrilled to see **T**ony. **T**ony

is glad to be in the city. They take a

taxicab to the **t**oy store.

There it is! There are many toys in the store

window. Tony cannot wait to get inside.

Tony sees the stuffed animals. There is

a **t**eddy bear. There is a tiny rabbit.

The stuffed **t**oys are soft to touch.

Tony finds a tambourine. He shakes and

hits the tambourine. Tony thinks it is

perfect! Aunt Tess turns the other way.

Aunt Tess sees the trucks. There is

a fire truck. There is a dump truck.

Tony wants a truck. He takes the

bright red and blue truck.

Aunt Tess buys the truck for Tony. Thank

you, Aunt Tess! It has been a great trip to

the toy store. Tony has had an excellent

time in the city.

Fun Facts

 Have you ever taken a ride in a taxicab? Taxicabs—also called *taxis* and *cabs*—are automobiles for hire. To hire a taxicab means to pay the taxi driver to take you somewhere. Usually a taxicab looks like a regular car that has been slightly changed. For example, a taxicab often has a radio so the driver can talk to the cab company and a light on the roof that turns on if the cab is for hire.

 Today, the teddy bear is one of the world's best-loved toys, but it was invented just a short time ago. Our cute, snuggly friends are only 100 years old! The teddy bear was named after Theodore "Teddy" Roosevelt, the 26th president of the United States. Teddy Roosevelt loved to hunt, but on one trip, or so the story goes, he refused to shoot a baby bear. A cartoon illustrating the event was printed throughout the country. Two toymakers in New York were inspired by the cartoon and the teddy bear was born!

To Read More

About the Letter T

Klingel, Cynthia. *Task Time: The Sound of T.* Chanhassen, Minn.: The Child's World, 2000.

About Taxicabs

Barracca, Debra, Sal Barracca, and Mark Buehner (illustrator). *The Adventures of Taxi Dog.* New York: Dial Books for Young Readers, 1990.

Grover, Max. *Max's Wacky Taxi Day.* San Diego: Browndeer Press/Harcourt Brace, 1997.

Wilson-Max, Ken. *Big Yellow Taxi.* New York: Scholastic, 1996.

About Teddy Bears

Alborough, Jez. *Where's My Teddy?.* Cambridge, Mass.: Candlewick Press, 1992.

McPhail, David. *The Teddy Bear.* New York: Henry Holt and Company, 2002.

Words with t

Words with T at the Beginning
take
takes
taking
tambourine
taxicab
teddy
terrific
Tess
thank
the
there
they
thinks
this
thrilled
time
tiny
to
Tony
touch
toy
toys
trip
truck
trucks
tune
turns

Words with T in the Middle
city
hits
let's
letter
other
postcard
store
stuffed
wants

Words with T at the End
about
at
aunt
bright
cannot
excellent
get
great
it
perfect
quilt
rabbit
soft
visit
wait

About the Authors

Cynthia Klingel has worked as a high school English teacher and an elementary teacher. She is currently the curriculum director for a Minnesota school district. Cynthia Klingel lives with her family in Mankato, Minnesota.

Robert B. Noyed started his career as a newspaper reporter. Since then, he has worked in communications and public relations for a Minnesota school district for more than fourteen years. Robert B. Noyed lives with his family in Brooklyn Center, Minnesota.